# Vera McLuckie
## and the
# Daydream Club

by Jane Evans
illustrated by Ruth Mutch

First published in 2017 in England by
Your Stories Matter

www.yourstoriesmatter.org
hello@yourstoriesmatter.org

Your Stories Matter is an imprint of Explainer HQ Ltd
of Halton Mill, Mill Lane, Lancaster, LA2 6ND, England.

This book is printed in the Dyslexie font, the typeface for people
with dyslexia, though we find it great for all children. Go to
www.dyslexiefont.com to find out more about the typeface.

Fonts used on the cover are courtesy of Khrys Bosland
and are available from www.dafont.com

This title is available for sale online and from loads of great
bookshops.

A bulk discount is available for educational institutions and
charitable organisations through Your Stories Matter.

British Library Cataloguing in Publication Data.
A catalogue record for this book is available from the British Library.

ISBN 978-1-909320-64-2

For all the "penguins" out there.

# 1. Monday blues

Vera hated Mondays. She also hated Wednesdays, Thursdays and Fridays. But she especially hated Mondays. And all because of one thing— school.

It was Monday morning, 7am. Vera's pink teddy bear alarm clock started to beep. Beep-beepity-beep, beep-beepity-beep. Vera woke slowly from a deep sleep and rubbed her eyes. She pulled the alarm clock out from underneath her pillow. It was a strange place for it to live, but the ticking noise really annoyed her. You could hardly hear it under her pillow, until it started to beepity-beep that is.

She pressed the black button, turning the alarm off. She gazed at the teddy bear face smiling at her. For a brief moment she didn't remember what day it was and smiled back. And then it dawned on her. "It's Monday," she groaned. Her heart sank. She felt her stomach churn and a wave of panic flooded over her.

Some Monday mornings she felt sick. Some she was sick. Other times she felt sad or worried. When things were really bad she was sick, sad and worried. That was usually when there was something new happening at school.

Or worse still a test. Or the time when she had to stand up in front of the whole class and give a talk on 'My favourite thing'. But today was just a normal 'feeling sick Monday'.

"Vera, love. Time to get up," her mum's sing-song voice breathed into the room.

'Light and airy'. Hmm, good words for mum thought Vera. Vera loved to think up ways to describe her mum. She's the most beautiful person in the whole wide world, Vera continued dreamily. She's small and delicate, like a doll. She has a ... a heart-shaped face, framed by the most amazing hair ... spirals of copper and gold that shine like leaves on an autumn day. Her face is creamy-white, her cheeks soft pink scattered with freckles. And her eyes ... her eyes are as green as my cat Biscuits' eyes.

Vera loved words—the way they painted pictures inside her head and made her thoughts come alive.

This particular morning Vera's mum, Martha, was wearing a multi-coloured silk kimono. It was a left over from the days before Vera came along, when she liked to visit exotic countries such as Africa and India. It makes her look like a butterfly, Vera daydreamed. A giant one, like the ones you find in the Amazon rainforest.

Vera could spend ages just thinking about her mum.

She made her feel so very, very safe and loved.

But ask Vera to describe herself, she would reply quietly and with a frown on her face, "Nothing much to say really. I wear red glasses. My mum chose them for me. And I only ever wear comfy clothes. Nothing scratchy. I am the smallest person in my class. Mum tells me I look like my dad, but I've never met him. I'm very clumsy. And I absolutely hate school. The end."

"It really is time to get up Vera dear. Chop, chop!" Her mum never shouted at her. But Vera could tell that this was the last warning she was going to get before she was dragged out of bed and arranged into her school uniform.

"M'up," mumbled Vera, rolling out of bed and falling onto the floor with a bump. Vera fell over a lot.

Now, Vera hadn't always hated school. Although she was never very good with new places or routines, she'd been pretty happy to start with.

"You're such a clever little girl Vera," her mum had whispered to her as she lay in bed the night before her first day. She'd been right up close to her ear, so close that Vera could feel the warmth of her breath. "There's so many great things to learn. You'll just love it," she had said stroking Vera's soft brown hair to reassure her.

But after a few weeks, Vera realised what school was all about. Really

all about. Before going to
school, Vera had loved to
learn and learn and learn.

Facts about animals. Facts
about plants. Facts about planets.
Trees. Flowers. Kings and
Queens. Faraway lands.
Facts about pretty much
anything.

"You're a walking
encyclopaedia, girl,"
Gran had cooed (Gran was her Number
One Fan.)

But school was different. There she
had to learn to read and write, do
maths, take part and join in—doing
her best at all times. Vera found it
exhausting. And terrifying. And very,
very hard. She had no idea that you

had to do all this before you got to learn any of the interesting stuff. Her handwriting was slow and messy. She felt slow and messy—and oh so stupid.

Most days her head ached with the amount she had to take in. She noticed everything. What the teachers were wearing. The colour of her classmates' bags. If anything had been changed around in her classroom. And that was even before the lessons began.

Some days she simply found it too much. The noise of the bells. The chatter. The lights. The movement. The doing one thing this moment, another thing the next. On those days she would just burst, and then cry and cry, and cry some more. On those days, when her head simply became too full, she just longed for peace and quiet and a cuddle with Biscuits her cat.

# 2. An extraordinary girl

*So now you've met Vera. It took her ages to eat her breakfast and get dressed that Monday morning. Her fingers fumbled over the buttons on her shirt and her school tie took six attempts to look barely presentable.*

*She really is worth getting to know though. You might think that she seems quite normal, maybe even a bit like you. But as we all know, there's no such thing as normal. And Vera is,*

well, no such thing as normal. In fact
she is quite

extraordinary

# 3. Friends, foes & maths

"Wait up guys!" Vera shouted as she lurched out of her mum's car. It was a tiny toy-like thing, rusty red and very, very old.

"A proper Mini," Martha liked to declare proudly, "before Minis became cool and not mini anymore."

Vera turned to blow a kiss to her mum, but she'd already disappeared, chugging off in a cloud of dirty

grey smoke. Vera spun round, heavy
rucksack on her back, straight
into Bethany Chalmers. Bethany
Chalmers—the coolest, most elegant,
cleverest, all round bestest being at
Acorn Bank Primary (perhaps even in
the whole of Oakchester).

"Vera McLuckie," Bethany sneered,
smoothing her perfect blonde plait
and brushing herself down as if trying
to remove all contact with Vera.

"Always in the way. Always such a ..." She paused to spit out the final word, "Mess."

Bethany ran a cold and critical eye over Vera, watching her as she pushed her shiny red glasses back into place.

Vera had just left the house looking near-perfect, approximately ten minutes ago. After her mum had retied her tie of course. But in that short space of time her shirt had come untucked. Her socks had fallen down. And her fine brown hair had begun to slip out of its daily ponytail.

"Run along and catch up with your special friends," jeered Bethany, as she looked down her beautiful little nose at Vera. As well as being cool,

elegant and clever, Bethany Chalmers
was also extremely horrible.

Vera slunk off, head down, and caught
up with Max and Harry, her two best
friends at school. In the world. In
the universe. Max Smyth and Harry
Brookwater. Max and Harry. Harry and
Max.

"Hey, it's Veraaaaaaaaa! Hi Vee!"
Harry gave Vera an enormous bear
hug, nearly knocking her over. Harry
was as big as Vera was small. She
often laughed telling people she was
actually a giant. But deep down she
hated being so much bigger than
everyone else in her
class.

There were two reasons why Harry was so big. Firstly, she just was. All of the Brookwaters were. Her mum, dad and two big brothers (Archie and Arthur) were enormous and could easily be spotted in any crowd. Secondly, she was a year older than the rest of Vera's class. When Vera had first met her she'd explained that her Mum and Dad had decided she could start school a year later to help her catch up with her 'dee-vel-hope-mint'.

Like Vera, Harry found writing and spelling hard. But while Vera loved to read, Harry hated it. "It doesn't make any sense," she'd complain, "the words just dance around on the page. They won't stay still long enough for me to work out what they say."

Now, you may be wondering at this point why Harry was called Harry. After all, she is a girl. Well, you see, as well as being very big, both her parents were very clever. So clever in fact that they were both Professors of Something-or-Other at the nearby university. So they decided to call her a very clever name. Arianna. But when you find writing and spelling as hard as Harry did, the name Arianna Brookwater had to go. And so she started to call herself Harry. Harry B to be precise.

In fact, it was her name that had first attracted Vera to Harry B. Vera had also been given a very long and tricky-to-spell name. Guinevere. Her mum, Martha, had studied Medieval Literature (that's very old books to

you and me) after she'd left school.
And so she'd desperately wanted
her only daughter to have the name of
a queen. So Guinevere it was.

How romantic, thought Martha. How
stupid, thought Vera. Vera had quickly
shortened her name when she started
school and realised just how long it
took her to write. She particularly
liked the fact that Harry often
shortened her name even further, to
Vee.

As soon as they reached the
playground, Vera, Max and Harry
bunched up and huddled around each
other making a tight little circle.

"I like your new tights," said Vera, looking down at Harry's legs. Vera noticed everything. "And Max, you OK?" Vera asked gently.

Max nodded. Max didn't speak very often. But when he did he spoke for ages, usually about his favourite things like computer games or numbers. Or his collection of timetables. He felt safe and calm with Vera and Harry. They just let him be himself and loved him for it. And that made him very happy indeed.

They also didn't try to knock his baseball cap off like all the other kids in his class. Max wore his baseball cap all the time. For the last 14 months, 3 weeks and 2 days to be precise. Even to bed. And in the bath.

His mum would prise it off him once a month so he could wash his hair.

The cap was bright green and had 'Don't worry, be happy!' written on it alongside a yellow smiley face. It was Max's lucky cap. He couldn't go anywhere without it perched on his head. It stopped him from pulling his hair out, which he did sometimes. Usually at school when he felt worried about something.

"Shall we meet up at Gran's bookshop again after school today?" asked

Vera. "I love it when we all spend time together," she paused and smiled. "Away from school, that is!"

Harry nodded enthusiastically. "Maybe you can help me with my homework again?" Harry looked at Vera and Max, her eyes pleading.

"I was kind of hoping that you guys would help me too!" laughed Vera.

"Agreed. Let's meet at 4pm," said Max. "Please don't be late though Vera." He looked at Vera very seriously for a moment, "It's such a waste of time when you're late. And I've got a new bus timetable I want to show you after we're done."

"It's a deal," said Vera. Harry beamed.

The school bell rang out, shrill and loud. "Time to go in," said Max.

"I hate that bell," said Vera covering her ears as the sound pulsed through her body.

"Race you!" shouted Harry, springing off at a trot.

But Max and Vera just trudged

behind, weighed down by their heavy school bags. And the thought of yet another day in Room 24 with Miss Richards.

☺☺☺

"Vera McLuckie! Stop daydreaming and get on with your work!"

It was now just after lunchtime and Miss Richards was at her desk busy marking last night's homework. The class was doing maths from the board.

Miss Richards was young, tall and slim with short, wispy blonde hair that stuck out around her enthusiastic face. She loved to teach. But she couldn't help getting frustrated with Vera and her daydreaming. Particularly when she knew just how bright she really was.

Maths was Vera's second least favourite subject, especially when she had to copy all the questions from the board before she could start answering them.

She'd managed two so far and had now forgotten what Miss Richards had asked her to do in the first place. So she'd drifted off into her own little world.

She liked her own little world. She felt happy there. She'd been looking out of the window and seen a seagull bobbing around in the sky, buffeted by the wind. She'd been wondering what it would be like to be a bird flying high in the sky.

Vera put her hand up timidly. "Please Miss. Can you remind me again what I have to do?" she asked in a small voice, hoping no one else would hear her.

"Honestly, Vera! I wish you would listen more and daydream less," tutted Miss Richards. "Maths. Questions 1 to 10," she snipped, "and then when you've finished you can choose a book to read. OK?"

Vera nodded and smiled a weak smile at Max and Harry. She thought she heard sniggering coming from the direction of Bethany Chalmers who sat on the table behind her. Her heart sank. Why can't I just be like everyone else, she thought? Why can I never remember what Miss Richards tells me for more than 30 seconds?

"Questions 1 to 10. Questions 1 to 10. Questions 1 to 10," Vera repeated,

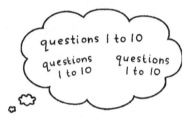

whispering to herself under her breath. But she couldn't stop thinking about the seagull in the sky outside the classroom, flying free. Oh to be 'free as a bird'.

And then her thoughts turned to

meeting Max and Harry after school at Gran's bookshop, the finest bookshop in the whole of Oakchester. Actually, it was the only bookshop in the whole of Oakchester.

They really needed a name for their club. After all, they'd been meeting at the bookshop for a couple of weeks now. So that made it official, right? Vera smiled and her eyes sparkled as an idea popped into her mind. Perhaps we could call it 'The Daydream Club' she thought.

Just then the bell rang for home time, jolting Vera back to the classroom. She covered her ears to block out the piercing noise and glanced down at her exercise book. She'd only reached Question 3.

# 4. Superteacher

You can probably tell that Vera, Harry and Max had a pretty tough time at school most days.

I'm sure you noticed way back at the beginning, when we first met Vera, that I missed out Tuesdays from the days-hated-by-Vera list. You see, Vera loved Tuesdays. In fact, all three of them loved Tuesdays. This was the day they all went to see Mrs Chalmers, for one whole hour. Each.

Vera thought Mrs Chalmers was the best teacher ever. She let Vera tell stories and got her to write them down. She didn't shout or interrupt or anything. No matter how long it took her.

Max liked her because she didn't mind if he wasn't looking her in the eye when he was talking to her about tricky things—like feelings.

Harry called her 'Superteacher' and suggested they get her a superhero cape for the end of term to thank her for being so great. As well as helping Harry with her reading, Mrs Chalmers was also Harry's swimming coach. Harry was a very, very good swimmer and a truly excellent artist. Her paintings and drawings were quite magnificent.

The funny thing—and you may have guessed this already—is that Mrs Chalmers was Bethany Chalmers' mum. Can you believe it? How can the kind, caring, understanding Mrs Chalmers have a daughter like Bethany?

But I'm talking too much again, and it's still only Monday. I'd better go for now and let you get on with the story. I'll catch up with you later though.

# 5. Dog-Eared Books

Vera, Harry and Max charged out of school, racing along, school bags joggling.

"Doesn't your Gran mind us all coming round to her bookshop after school Vee?" asked Harry.

"Nah," puffed Vera, out of breath. They were all still running and Vera was struggling to keep up with the others. She stopped.

So did Max and Harry.

"She likes it," explained Vera. "It's not like she's ever got any customers anyway. And she says we bring 'the joy of childhood' back into her life."

"Please explain what that means," said Max. He was working hard at being able to understand the way that other people talked and what they really meant when they said things. At least with Vera and Harry he knew he could always ask without being made to feel silly.

"It means," said Vera kindly, "that she's lonely ever since my Grandad died and that she loves our company, and our chats."

"Oh, I see," said Max.

Vera's Gran was indeed lonely. She missed Vera's Grandad terribly. He'd died two years ago and her second-hand bookshop 'Dog-Eared Books' really didn't have that many customers.

"Maybe it's the name?" suggested Vera's mum one day when Gran was complaining how quiet things had been lately. "You know, it makes folk think that everything's a bit, well, shabby."

"That's the whole point, Martha dear," said Gran. "It is after all for second-hand books.

It might also have had something to do with where the bookshop was.

Dog-Eared Books was tucked down one of Oakchester's many small side alleys. This particular alley was beside the fish shop in the centre of the village. The alley was always dark, no matter what time of year it was. And it always smelled of fish.

"Poo-ee!" shouted Harry as they rounded the corner into the alleyway. "Hold your noses guys!"

"It's not that bad," said Vera turning the worn brass handle on the shop's door. The open sign swung on its frayed length of string and the shop bell tinkled as they all trooped in.

"Hi Gran!" shouted Vera. "It's only us."

Gran shuffled through from the back of the shop, her wild grey curls flying loose and long behind her. When she was younger, Gran had looked just like Vera's mum—very beautiful, only much messier.

"Vera!" she beamed hugging her tightly to her chest. She ruffled Vera's already untidy hair, nearly knocking her glasses off her face. "How's my gorgeous girl today?"

"OK," said Vera.

"How was school?" Gran asked, a bit more cautiously this time.

"The usual," sighed Vera.

Gran smiled a knowing smile. "Never mind love, you're here now. On you go through to the back room. The heater is on and I've just set out some juice and biscuits for you coming." She hugged Vera close and turned to Harry and Max. "And how are my other two favourite people?"

"Great, now I'm here!"
beamed Harry.

"I am very well thank you, Milly,"
said Max rather awkwardly, having
practised the line many times before.
He was the only one of them who
dared call Vera's Gran 'Milly'. "Why
not? It is her name," he would simply
explain.

They all trotted through to the back
room, avoiding piles upon piles of
books as they went.

Vera's Gran had been a not-very-good
librarian when she was younger. She
was always a bit too messy and untidy
for the grand libraries of the big cities
and towns—forever making mistakes
and getting into trouble.

So she'd decided to open her own bookshop and Dog-Eared Books was born. It really was a good name for the shop because everything smelled a bit musty, like an old dog. Not helped by the fact that there really was an old dog in the shop, called Shakespeare.

Shakespeare looked just like Gran, with long shaggy grey hair. He spent most of his days on a large pile of blankets in a box underneath an old wooden desk in the back room.

Vera's Gran knew where every single book was in the shop, which was pretty amazing. Especially when the shop looked like someone had just thrown a whole load of books at a whole load of shelves and hoped for the best. Maybe that was another reason not many people visited Dog-Eared Books?

The back room was as jumbled up as the rest of the shop. Boxes, bags and old bits of furniture were crammed into the tiny space, all covered with a thin film of dust.

Vera, Harry and Max sat down at the old wooden desk. Vera kicked off her shoes and started warming her feet on Shakespeare's back. He gruffed in pleasure.

"Homework time then," sighed Vera as she picked up a chocolate biscuit from the plate that Gran had set out for them.

"Yes," agreed Max, "4:00pm until 4:30pm. Let's give ourselves half an hour," he added for Vera's benefit. She was terrible at telling the time.

"The usual?" asked Harry hopefully.

The usual was this. Max helped Vera with maths. Vera helped Harry with her reading. Harry and Vera helped Max with writing about feelings, and other tricky things that people do.

"I've got to describe someone today," said Max, "which would normally be so easy because I notice everything. But this time I have to write lots of detail about what they say and think. Using adjectives and stuff. How on earth am I meant to do that?" he said staring helplessly at Vera and Harry.

But thirty minutes later the juice
was drunk, the biscuits were eaten
and Vera, Harry and Max had finished
their homework.

"Time up," said Max.

Everyone let out a huge sigh of relief.
Even Shakespeare joined in from under
the table.

"Good teamwork," said Harry, giving a
double thumbs up sign.

"Excellent," beamed Vera. "I hate
homework, especially maths."

She paused, "I've got a great idea for
what we could do next though. You
know how we've been doing this for a
couple of weeks now. Well, I thought

we're now kind of an official club-type thing. And so ..."

"But first," interrupted Max, wiggling excitedly in his chair, "I have to show you my new bus timetable!"

Now when Max said he had to do something, he really did have to do it. Right there and then. Otherwise he would get totally stressed and tug at his hair under his cap.

He pulled the timetable out of his school bag and smoothed it out on the desk. He was very careful not to get chocolate biscuit crumbs stuck to it.

"It's for the 274 in London. It's so

great," he said quickly, eyes gleaming with enthusiasm. "It goes all the way from Hyde Park to Angel Islington and back again. Look!"

"Super," said Harry, rolling her eyes at Vera.

Vera tried to kick her under the table but missed and got poor Shakespeare instead. Thankfully he was too sound asleep to notice.

"And do you know what the best thing is Vera? Do you?" Max was getting very excited now. "It goes to the zoo. The actual London Zoo!"

"Cool!" said Vera, genuinely interested. She loved animals more than anything. "That's brilliant Max.

A real keeper for your collection."
She smiled kindly at her friend,
watching him carefully fold the
timetable back into a neat rectangle.
Something she would never have been
able to do.

Vera took a deep breath and started
again, feeling slightly awkward. She
hoped she wouldn't be interrupted this
time round. "So, the club-type thing
that I was kind of talking about there
before Max got his timetable out ..."
She so desperately wanted to tell her
friends about her brilliant idea. "Well
I've been thinking about it all day in
class."

"That explains why you kept on
getting into trouble Vee!" laughed
Harry.

"Shh! Let her speak. It's Vera's turn now," said Max, ever fair.

"Sorrr-eee," chimed Harry.

"So yes, uhm. We've been coming here for a couple of weeks now, to do our homework and talk about the stuff we like. And so, uhm, I wondered if we could make it into an official club. Just us three. To do our homework and talk about our special stuff. And, uhm ..." she paused. "I thought we could call it The Daydream Club?"

"Oh Vera! That is perfect," exclaimed Harry. She slapped the table with both her hands. So loudly that Shakespeare, woken from his deep sleep, jumped in fright and howled. He slouched off to another pile of blankets stuffed in a heap of old cardboard boxes on the other side of the room. "That is so you. You are such a daydreamer."

"What do you think Max?" asked Vera.

"It's good," said Max nodding. "I like it. I'll draw up some rules on timekeeping and stuff and maybe put together some membership booklets." He paused to think, "I'll do it on the computer tonight."

"Brilliant," said Vera. "Same time, same place tomorrow?"

# 6. The Daydream Club takes off

Tuesday. The best day of the week. But only once assembly was over.

Vera, Harry and Max stood side by side, fourth line from the back in the school hall. It was a rather shabby space, a bit like the rest of Acorn Bank Primary. Pale green paint flaking off the walls and bright fluorescent lights that Vera hated. They made her eyes hurt and her head ache.

"Good morn-ing, Mis-ter Gib-son!"
they chorused as the Headmaster
walked in and took his position at the
centre of the stage in front of them.

Mr Gibson was a tall man, with
dark hair and a matching beard. He
had a kind smile and a gentle voice.
Until, that is, anyone in the school
misbehaved. Then his smile would
quickly turn into a stern frown and his
voice into a bark. He got particularly
annoyed if he caught anyone calling
him by his nickname, 'The Gibbon'.

"Good morning everyone," he smiled.
Obviously no one had got up to any
mischief so far, as he was clearly in
a very good mood. "It gives me great
pleasure when the pupils of Acorn
Bank Primary do something to make

us all proud. Today is one of those days," he exclaimed, beaming at the children gathered before him.

"Last week, three of our pupils took part in the Oakchester Junior Maths Challenge.

And one of them, Bethany Chalmers,
came first. Please join me in
congratulating Bethany on her
incredible
achievement."

Mr Gibson started to clap heartily. He beckoned Bethany to join him on the stage to collect the shiny gold medal he was holding in his hand.

Vera, Harry and Max groaned and clapped as slowly and quietly as they could possibly get away with.

"She always wins everything," moaned Harry under her breath so none of the teachers would hear her. "And she always looks so smug about it."

"I've never won anything," sighed Vera as she watched Bethany smile confidently, soaking up the praise from her fellow pupils. Vera's shoulders drooped and she suddenly felt very, very small indeed. Much smaller than usual.

"S'OK Vee. Our time will come," said
Harry putting an arm around Vera.
She tried to put her other arm around
Max but he shrugged her off. He
wasn't one for hugs.

"Maybe," sighed Vera even more
heavily as she watched Bethany
Chalmers come down from the stage
and back to her seat. Vera was sure
that she caught Bethany sneering at
her and her heart sank further.

It took ages for Vera to get from the
school hall to Mrs Chalmers' class
after assembly. She felt like a burst
balloon and dragged her feet and her
school bag all the way through the
dingy corridors. Corridors that were

painted an even grubbier shade of
green than the school hall. Thankfully
for Vera, they were not as brightly lit.

"Vera, my dear! Come in, come in.
How lovely to see you," Mrs Chalmers
greeted Vera with a beaming smile as
she opened the door.

Now, Mrs Chalmers smiled a lot. No
matter what time of day you saw her
in school. No matter what kind of day
she'd had. She was always smiling.

She was the happiest person Vera
knew—second only to Harry. Maybe
it's because her classroom is so sunny
and neat and tidy. Not at all like the
rest of the school thought Vera. So
she'd asked her one day.

"It's because I absolutely love my
job," Mrs Chalmers had explained.
"You see, I get to work with the
most interesting, most creative, most
intelligent kids in the school," she'd
said. But Vera hadn't really believed
her.

Mrs Chalmers' name was Belinda.
Vera knew this because she'd
overheard another teacher talking to
her one day—and Vera was very good
at remembering things like names.

And today Belinda was very excited. "I've got great news for you Vera," she said in her soft breathy voice that Vera loved so much. "There's a short story competition coming up at the end of the month for junior schools in Oakchester."

Vera nodded, listening carefully.

"And I'd like you to enter one of your stories. They're ever so good Vera. Quite unique. I think you have a real chance."

Vera's eyes widened and her breath quickened. "My stories? You're kidding, aren't you? I thought we just did them in here to practise my writing. I can't write a story for a competition. I can't even write properly."

"You don't have to write it. Not by hand at least," explained Mrs Chalmers gently.

Vera looked confused.

"What I mean is, we can work together to plan it out if you want. Then you can type it up on the computer. All entries are to be typed anyway."

The panic in Vera's eyes began to lessen. Her shoulders relaxed and her breathing returned to normal. "Phew!" Vera sighed. A small smile began to creep around the edges of her mouth. "Are you sure? Me? Enter a competition?"

"Yes, I'm sure Vera. I know this
sounds scary but there is absolutely
no need to be frightened. I believe
in you and I know you're capable
of great things. I just need you to
believe that too."

"OK," said Vera slowly, beginning to
take it all in, "I'll see what I can do."

Vera couldn't wait to tell Harry and
Max her news. One of her stories, in a
competition! But what if nobody liked
it? She began to panic.

"Of course they will!" enthused
Harry. "Your stories are always fab!"

It was after school and the three

friends had taken their places in the back room of Dog-Eared Books.

"You've got an incredible imagination Vera," agreed Max. "I don't always understand your stories but they are very good," he added, nodding reassuringly to himself as much as to Vera.

Shakespeare gave a gruff of agreement from his place under the table.

"Shall we give it a go now?" asked Vera.

Harry and Max looked at her, slightly confused.

"I mean, I've kind of got this idea. For the story that is. I've been dreaming it up all afternoon while I was supposed to have been catching up with yesterday's maths. Miss Richards will be furious when she realises how little I've done. Again." Vera frowned but carried on, "What do you think? Would you like to hear it? Harry? Max?"

"Course we would!" they chorused.

"No homework tonight Vera, so the Daydream Club's time today is all yours," said Max as he placed three small booklets on the table in front of them.

On the front of each booklet, in large green (Max's favourite colour) writing, were the letters 'DDC'. And below them was a photograph of the three

friends, grinning widely, taken one
sunny day last year at the seaside.

"It's the membership booklets, as
promised," added Max. "There's one
for each of us. And there's some club
rules inside too. Well, there's only
one actually." He gave Vera a knowing

look. "About timekeeping. But we can always add more if we want to."

"Thanks Max. You're the best," beamed Harry.

Harry and Max settled back in their seats and waited for Vera to begin.

The back room felt cosy and welcoming. It had been chillier than normal outside. One of those days in late spring when it seems like winter has returned for one last visit.

Vera's mum had made her wear a duffel coat and one of her hand-knitted hat and scarf sets that she loved to make so much. Vera thought it made her look even more like a geek than normal. But she wore it anyway

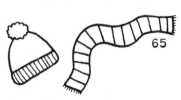

as she loved the softness of the special wool her mum always used.

Before they'd arrived, Gran had put an ancient fan heater in the back room and turned it on full blast, much to Shakespeare's joy. The gentle buzz of the heater, combined with the warmth of the air it blew out, began to make the friends feel very relaxed. And quite sleepy.

"So I'll begin," said Vera.

"Does it start with 'Once upon a time'?" asked Harry, jokingly.

"No. It does not Harry. Stop interrupting," said Vera. "Why don't you just close your eyes and listen? Then I won't have to look at you looking at me. You'll put me off."

So Harry and Max did as they were told and Vera began. As she talked, Vera could feel herself becoming warmer and warmer. The buzz of the heater began to fill her senses. Her eyelids became too heavy to keep open and her body began to feel lighter and lighter. Lighter than air. So light in fact that she felt like she was flying—like the seagull she'd seen only yesterday out of Miss Richard's classroom window.

Suddenly, she began to feel a chilly wind in her face, ruffling her hair and her clothes. Vera opened one eye. And then the other.

Oh. My. Goodness! What. On. Earth?

Vera tried to speak but the wind made it difficult for her to get the words out. So did the fact that she was flying! Actually flying. Arms outstretched, proper flying, up high. So high that the cars and people below looked like toys.
Flying. Through a perfect blue sky, with white fluffy clouds. Past soaring seagulls. Past ... wait a minute, she thought, it can't be.

"Alright Vee?" came a familiar voice. It was Harry, flying right up close to her now, with a rather terrified–

looking Max by her side. "Is this all part of the story then?"

"Gruff," said Shakespeare, who'd appeared along Vera's other side, ears flapping behind him, as he too flew effortlessly through the air.

# 7. Flying

*It's me again. You know, the person telling the story. Just thought I'd pop back and ask you a question.*

*Have you ever flown before? Proper flying that is, not in an aeroplane, a helicopter, a glider or a hot-air balloon. Not even that feeling you get when you jump off a very high thing or dive into a swimming pool. No, I mean proper flying. Through the sky, like a bird. Like Vera, Harry and Max. And*

*Shakespeare of course.*

*Well let me tell you. It's like nothing you've ever felt. It's a feeling of lightness. Being able to move through the sky like you would if you were running the fastest you could on land, but faster. It's the most amazing feeling ever, ever, ever.*

*How do I know? Well, we'll come to that later. But just let me tell you that while flying is one of the most incredible things you'll ever do, landing is a bit trickier.*

# 8. A trip to the zoo

"Oooooph!" said Vera as she hit
the ground heavily. She tried to run
as she landed but only managed a
slightly out of control jog before she
fell over (in soft sand luckily). After
a couple of roly-polys she came to
a stop, stood up and dusted herself
down. She hated sand and all its itchy
scratchiness.

"Weee heee! Woop! Woop! Woop!
Watch out below!" yelled Harry as

she swooped in managing to land far more gracefully than Vera. "That was awesome!"

"Actually, I feel a bit sick," disagreed Max as he landed beside them with a thud, bottom first. His face was as ghostly green as the walls in Acorn Bank Primary. "And a bit sore," he said as he rubbed his rear-end with one hand and adjusted his cap with the other. It was a bit of a miracle that cap had stayed on at all.

"Yeh," agreed Harry, "I know where you're coming from with the sick thing. It might have something to do with that awful smell. It's just like the alleyway outside your Gran's bookshop Vera, isn't it? Fish-eeee. Yeuch isn't it Vee? Vera?"

But Vera wasn't listening. She'd got up and begun to wander around, shaking sand out of her clothes as she went.

Shakespeare, who had landed better than any of them (perhaps four legs are better than two, at least for landing) sniffed around beside her, ears up.

"Where on earth are we?" she muttered, half to herself, half to Shakespeare.

Max interrupted her thoughts. "Um, Vera. I'm pretty sure I didn't imagine it but I think I saw the Number 274 bus before I landed. You remember the timetable I showed you yesterday? The bus that goes to London Zoo?

So I can only work out that's where we are— London Zoo!"

"But if we're at the zoo, where are all the animals? Not to mention all the people who come to see them?" asked a bewildered Harry.

"It's because we're in my story," muttered Vera to herself.

"It's because we're in my story," she said, clearer this time, confirming her thoughts to Harry and Max. "This isn't real. We're in story land. My story land. A land where I can make anything happen. A land where the story controls what you see, hear and think."

"Story what?" exclaimed Harry.

"Vera, I don't believe such a place exists," stated Max. "Otherwise, don't you think we would have learned about it at school?"

"Well how do you explain that?" said Vera, pointing to three penguins who were fast approaching them. Nothing out of the ordinary, except for the fact that they were waving. And talking.

"Welcome! Welcome, my dear friends!" they heard the first penguin say enthusiastically. He was bounding

towards them at a brisk pace, a little ahead of the other two who followed at a slower waddle. His red eyes gleamed in the sunshine and the yellow and black tufts on his head bounced as he trotted along.

Rockhopper thought Vera to herself. Or perhaps a Macaroni? Although he does look a bit too short for a Macaroni. Definitely a Rockhopper then, she decided.

Now, as you know, Vera loved animals. All animals. And she knew a lot about pretty much every one. Especially penguins. She'd studied her Big Book of Penguins at home in her room for hours on end, so was very good at telling which ones were which.

But the two behind, she wondered.
Bit bigger. Pinkish faces. Humboldts
maybe? Yes.

Vera jolted out of her thoughts and
reminded herself of her manners.
"Hello Mr Rockhopper," she
responded confidently, "and greetings
Humboldts!" she ended with a
flourish.

"Greetings—who on earth says that
Vera?" spluttered Harry, who'd
joined Vera by now and was holding
on tightly to Shakespeare. (In case
he decided to do more than sniff the
penguins.)

Vera dug her in the ribs with her sharp
elbow.

"Greetings to you too!" the Humboldts spoke together.

"Okay, obviously penguins say 'Greetings' then," mumbled Harry.

"And well done for getting our species correct first time," piped-up the smaller of the two. "Not many humans can tell us apart, they just think of us as penguins. Or, worse still, black and white birds. As if we were all simply the same." The Humboldts both shook their heads as if they were remembering something sad.

"But first things first. Please allow me to introduce ourselves," interrupted the Rockhopper in a shrill voice. "My name is Ricky and my good friends here are Henry and Helen," he

Henry    Helen    Ricky

said pointing his beak at each of the
Humboldts in turn.

Henry and Helen each waved a flipper
as their names were spoken.

"You can tell us apart by the spots
on our chests," added Helen. "I've got
more than Henry. See?"

They both puffed out their little white
chests to illustrate. "And I talk more
than you Henry, don't I?" said Helen.

Henry just smiled and nodded.

"And we're a lot more chilled out than old Ricky over there," she pointed her flipper at the Rockhopper and giggled.

"Very pleased to meet you. I'm Vera," replied Vera with a small wave. "I'm the one with the glasses. Max is the one in the hat. And Harry is ..."

"I'm the really tall one!" laughed Harry. "And together we make up the Daydream Club," she concluded, smiling at Vera and Max.

"Wonderful, just wonderful!" nodded Ricky in agreement, clapping his flippers together with great enthusiasm. "I often find it hard to tell you humans apart. There are always so many of you here every day,

just standing there looking at us. So
you all begin to look the same after
a while. But as we penguins know,
it's not what you look like that really
matters, is it?"

The Humboldts both smiled and
nodded wisely.

"No, it's what's inside that matters.
That and knowing what you're good
at," said Helen in her soothing voice.

"And what are you good at?" asked
Max as he shuffled forwards to stand
beside Vera and Harry, still rubbing
his aching bottom. He liked the
penguins, particularly Ricky with his
friendly chat and excellent manners.
He seemed to have completely
accepted the fact they were now

having a full-blown conversation with
three penguins.

"Swimming, of course!" exclaimed
Ricky. "Shall we show you?"

And with that the three penguins
began to head off in the direction
of the crystal clear pool in front of
them.

# 9. Penguins

"How fast do you think they're going Vee?" asked Harry. The three friends watched in awe as Ricky, Henry and Helen sped through the water like little black and white bullets—leaving behind a trail of shiny silver bubbles.

"Not that fast really," said Vera. "The pool isn't that big, so they can't get up to their top speeds. Did you know that Humboldts can go as fast as 30 miles per hour in open water?"

"Wowee!" exclaimed Harry. "Now that is fast. Imagine if I could swim like that. How proud would Mrs Chalmers be? I'd win every medal in Oakchester for sure."

"And that's called porpoising," Vera said pointing to the penguins as they leaped out of the water mid-swim, grabbing a breath before they dived back under.

"They're so graceful," said Max watching carefully. "It's funny because on land they look so clumsy and uncomfortable."

"A bit like me," added Vera as she twirled round and stumbled over Shakespeare who had crouched down beside her, his eyes fixed on the water.

"Sorry Shakespeare!" she said as she gave his head a quick ruffle.

"That's alright," came a gruff reply.

"Crikey, not you as well" exclaimed Vera. "Shakespeare, the talking dog. Hah!"

"That's another one to add to our list of strange-things-that-have-happened then," laughed Harry. "I must say that this story land of yours is totally bizarre Vee, but I am loving it."

Vera, Harry and Max followed the penguins' every movement as they glided, spun, jumped and flipped their way through their routine. They finished by speeding round in a gigantic loop then—heading straight for shore at speed—propelled themselves out of the water. Helen and Henry first, followed by Ricky with one of his signature hops. They landed with a plop at the feet of the three friends.

"Da-da!" said Ricky with a small bow, his red eyes brighter than ever, shining with pride. "So what did you think of the show?"

"Amazing!" chimed Vera, Harry and Max.

"Quite the most amazing thing I've ever seen," added Vera. "I mean, I've seen penguins swimming before at the zoo and on the television and everything. But I've never been this close or really thought about how incredible you are," she praised.

"Thank you. Thank you, my kind friends," said Ricky with another of his familiar hops. "We penguins are amazing birds aren't we?"

"But not everyone thinks so," muttered Henry as he hung his head sadly, his beak pointing downwards almost touching his soft spotted belly.

"What do you mean?" asked Vera. "Everyone loves you. Think how many visitors come to see you at the zoo every year."

"I'm not talking about people," said the sad Humboldt. "They love us because of what we are. I'm talking about the other birds at the zoo. The owls. The hawks. But particularly that really annoying toucan. And that

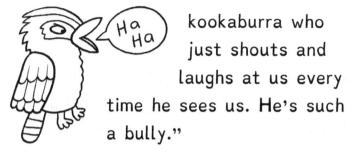 kookaburra who just shouts and laughs at us every time he sees us. He's such a bully."

"But why?" asked Max. "I don't understand."

"Because we're different," smiled Helen sadly, her pale pink face flushing a deep shade of red. "We're not like other birds, you see. They can fly."

"We even call our wings flippers," Helen continued. "And so they think that because we can't fly there's ..." she took a deep breath, "that there's something wrong with us. That we're stupid. And so they tease us."

"But that's just crazy," said Harry. "I love to swim and I've been to competitions all over and watched some of the best swimmers around. And no one, not one person I know, can swim as well as you penguins."

"Who cares about flying anyway?" Harry continued. "We did it on our way here and while it was incredible and great fun and stuff, I really think it's overrated. And landing is very messy indeed. But swimming, the type of swimming you do, that's one of the coolest things I've ever seen."

"Thank you! Thank you for your kindness," chipped in Ricky. "I keep on telling my friends here that we need to keep our minds on what we are good at and forget about what the other birds say. We're never going to be able to fly, so why even worry about it. Let's just concentrate on what makes us special. I'd like to see that horrible kookaburra try to swim!" he laughed.

"Well said, Ricky!" agreed Harry.

The Humboldts began to beat their flippers in appreciation.

Max smiled.

But Vera simply stared. And stared. And stared some more.

"Veraaaaa? Oh Veraaaaa?" Harry said poking her in the ribs.

Even Shakespeare joined in with one gruff of "Vera!" as he started to paw her leg.

"What? Oh yes. Sorry. Absolutely," agreed Vera shaking her head. "It's just that it all makes sense now. Everything. It really does. I know why I'm here. Why we're all here. Why I'm telling this story. It all makes complete and utter sense."

"Vera," interrupted Max, "it may make complete sense to you but trust me when I say it makes no sense whatsoever to us. So please explain."

"Of course. Of course," Vera went on, still staring off into space. "You see. It's us. Vera, Harry and Max. We're penguins!"

"Umm, Vee? This is getting weird now," said Harry, "I'm pretty sure the last time I looked I definitely wasn't a penguin. Unless you've written that into your story somehow." Harry glanced down quickly to make sure that she was still in fact Harry and then turned her gaze to Vera as if demanding an explanation.

Even the three penguins were giving Vera a quizzical look.

It worked. Vera jolted out of her dreamlike state and smiled at her two friends—a slow, steady, calm smile. Then she smiled at the penguins.

"All my life I've felt different," she

went on to explain. "I've always felt like I'm not as good as everyone else. Not as clever. Not as sporty. Not as ... well ... you know, just different."

"But then I met you guys," she reached out and put her arms around Harry and Max (Max didn't shrink away this time). "I realised I wasn't the only one who didn't fit in. I wasn't alone."

"But it's not until today, just now watching these penguins swim, that I realised that we're just like them. We might be the odd ones out. The ones who need extra help with reading, writing and getting on with other people. You know, just the ordinary stuff."

"But we're all extraordinary in our own way. We all have our own talents. We are all good at something. Really good at it."

"I'm great at storytelling," she continued modestly, grinning at Harry and Max. "You Harry, well you're the best swimmer in Oakchester for sure, and your drawings are just brilliant. And Max, you're a maths genius and a wizard on the computer."

By now, Harry and Max were nodding in total agreement.

"And these are the things that make us special—in a good way, not the way that Bethany Chalmers says it." Vera stopped speaking, though her grin didn't stop widening.

There was a long silence and then Max piped up. "Wow, you're right Vera. We are penguins!"

Harry sniffed. "I think I've got something in my eye, Vee." Vera could see that Harry's eyes were welling up with tears.

"That was just beautiful. Beautiful!" Ricky the Rockhopper began to clap.

"Bravo! Bravo!" chorused Helen and Henry joining in the applause.

"I think you've got it, my girl. I think you now have what you need," Ricky said as he hopped lightly over to Vera.

He reached down, scrabbled around in the sand, and picked up a smooth white pebble with his beak. Lifting his head gently, he nodded at her.

"Hold out your hand," said Helen softly.

Vera held out her hand and Ricky dropped the pebble into her palm.

"For you," he said with a small bow, "a fellow penguin."

Vera's fingers curled round the comforting coolness of the pebble. And as they did, she began to feel a now familiar sense of lightness fill her entire body. Once again, she began to lift up into the air and watched as the penguins got smaller and smaller the higher she went. She could still make out their little faces, upturned to the sky, as she waved them farewell.

# 10. Really real

*You see? I told you Vera was*
*extraordinary, didn't I? Way back at*
*the beginning. But I bet you didn't*
*realise she was that extraordinary.*
*That she could make herself and her*
*friends fly. Or make penguins (or dogs*
*for that matter) talk just by telling a*
*story. That she could actually make it*
*happen.*

*Not like other storytellers.*
*Their books can take you off*

to a million different places, that's true. But you know at the end of it all, when you finish the last chapter, close your book and turn off your light to go to sleep, that it was only a story. That it wasn't really real. That it was just someone else's imagination you'd dipped into for a while.

Well, unfortunately for Vera, that's exactly what Harry and Max thought of her story.

# 11. The pebble

"Crikey Vera! That was incredible!"

Vera opened her eyes to find herself back in Gran's bookshop. Back to the buzz of the heater as it filled the room with warm air. Back to Harry and Max sitting opposite her, staring at her—hard. So was Shakespeare for that matter.

"That was the best story ever," continued Harry. "Mrs Chalmers is right Vee, you do have a real talent for storytelling. It all felt so ..."

"Real," Max quickly finished Harry's sentence, as he adjusted his baseball cap. He had a quizzical look on his face. "Everything felt so real. Flying. The penguins. Even the smell of fish. How did you do it?"

"I ... I ... I don't know," Vera stammered. "It all just came out. When I closed my eyes, the story just came out. I felt every single bit of it too, you know," Vera added in a whisper beginning to doubt herself. Beginning to wonder if it had been just a story after all.

Confused, she looked hard at her friends for answers. Her eyes moved between Harry and Max, studying them. As she did, she realised they had no idea what had happened. For them everything had already returned to normal. Even Shakespeare had clearly dismissed his recent flying-talking experience as simply another doggy dream. He had flopped back into his bed and fallen quickly asleep.

"It was magic. Pure magic Vera! What a great way to start the Daydream Club. What a brilliant story for your competition. The pictures you painted with your words were so clear. I feel like I could easily draw each of the penguins!" Harry was looking super-excited now.

"It is a great story, isn't it?" Vera set aside her feelings of doubt for a moment and a small smile of something special crept across her face. She knew this smile, this feeling. This was the feeling she got when she believed in herself. When she felt confident. Like when she was with Mrs Chalmers. Or when she got to talk about animals and all the other stuff she knew so much about. Real or not, her story was good. In fact, it was great.

There was a gentle knock at the door of the back room and Gran shuffled in. She wore a long, loose-fitting dress, all silky and a jumble of patterns and colours. There were two ribbon ties at the neckline made of gold thread. At the end of each of the ties was a tiny

bell so that Gran jingled whenever
she moved. Vera loved this dress. The
feel of it. The tinkly noise it made
when her Gran walked. And, of course,
because it was Gran's.

"Having fun, my dearies?" asked Gran
in her warm voice.

Vera, Harry and Max nodded and
looked at each other. The kind of look
you give your friends when you've been
caught doing something you shouldn't
have been doing.

"I don't want to spoil the party,"
added Gran seeing the look on their
faces, "but have you seen the time?"

They looked through the door to the
front shop. There was an enormous,

dusty old clock hanging shakily from a
rusty nail that stuck out of one of the
bookshelves.

"Six o'clock!" shrieked Harry. "My mum's going to kill me. I should have been home an hour ago!"

"I hardly think she's going to kill you," Max said calmly, shaking his head. "But we really better go as we are very late."

"It's OK, my dears," soothed Gran. "I've just phoned your parents to let them know you're on your way and that you've been here safe and sound all the time. Now wrap up warm before you head off home. There's a real chill in the air tonight."

Harry and Max bundled themselves into their coats.

"See you tomorrow Vera," said Max.

"This was just brilliant," grinned Harry, grabbing the last biscuit from the plate as they headed out. The shop bell tinkled as they slammed the door behind them.

"You sit there, my love," said Vera's Gran. "I'm just going to shut up shop then I'll take you home to mine for tea. Your mum has got to work a bit late again tonight, so I thought I'd make your favourite—sausages, rice and peas. She'll pick you up on her way home," she said reassuringly.

Vera's mum was always working late. Martha was a social worker in Oakchester. "Never enough hours in the day, never enough people to do all the work," Martha would laugh when

Vera asked her why she was having to spend more and more nights having tea with Gran.

"There's always someone worse off than yourself Vera," Martha had explained. "And it's my job to help them." Sometimes Vera wished her mum was around a bit more to help her.

Vera could hear Gran emptying the money out of the cash register in the front shop to put in the safe for the night. Not that there would be much money to put in as today had been another slow day at Dog-Eared Books.

She glanced over at Shakespeare who was snoring soundly on his bed. She began to get all her things together, ready for heading off. For Vera, this meant cramming everything into her school bag in a messy crumpled heap.

As she pulled on her duffel coat, the sleeve caught something on the table. It rolled off and clattered to the floor. Vera bent her head down to see what it was. There, lying beside Shakespeare, was a smooth white pebble. She gasped and reached to pick it up.

It felt cool to touch and fitted perfectly and comfortably into the palm of her hand.

"Ricky!" she breathed excitedly. "So you were real. I knew it. I just knew it!"

# 12. Detention

Vera simply couldn't get penguins out of her head. Penguins, penguins, penguins. Rockhoppers and Humboldts. Ricky, Helen and Henry. She'd thought about them every waking moment (and most moments in her sleep) since last Tuesday.

In school, she'd sit at her desk and remember every single detail of what had happened as she daydreamed her way through class—playing it over and over in her mind. Bringing the pictures to life, big and bright and loud like a fabulous movie you just want to watch again and again. Flying—cool. Talking penguins—so, so cool. And the not-so-small fact that she, Vera McLuckie, had made her story come to life—absolutely amazing.

"Vera McLuckie!" Vera jolted back to the real world. Back to Room 24, her desk, and to Miss Richards.

"Crikey, she's in trouble now," said Harry, elbowing Max in the ribs.

Miss Richards was standing right in front of Vera, her eyes fixed hard on her workbook. "This is the third time today, Vera. And the hundredth time this week. It's simply not good enough, not good enough at all," she said sternly, nodding down at the blank pages in front of her.  "Particularly when you haven't even started your maths for today. Really Vera. Perhaps you'd like to share with the class exactly what you were daydreaming about?"

Vera could hear her heart pounding in her ears. Her pale cheeks blushed a bright shade of crimson and she could feel the palms of her hands go sticky with sweat.

She kept her eyes down, looking hard at her desk. Trying not to make eye contact with anyone, particularly not Miss Richards. Trying not to hear Bethany Chalmers snigger and whisper to her friend, "She's in real trouble now, just watch."

"Or perhaps you'd like to stay behind after school today for detention?"

Vera looked up to see Miss Richards raise her left eyebrow, the corners of her mouth turning up in a small but surprising smile. She was pretty sure Miss Richards gave her a tiny wink as well.

"Ummm," Vera began, ramming her clammy hands into her saggy cardigan pockets for comfort. There. There was the pebble, safe where her fingers could find it. Where she could feel its smoothness and turn it over and over again. And as she did she heard Ricky's shrill little voice echo in her ears, "We need to keep our minds on what we're good at."

"Sure, detention would be great. Thanks," mumbled Vera, nodding seriously, half to Miss Richards, half to the sound of Ricky's voice in her head.

Bethany and her friends began to giggle.

Harry shot them a look that said 'Drop dead!'

☹😐☺

When the bell rang for the end of the day, Vera stayed in her seat watching the rest of her class  pack up their bags and leave in single file.

"Later Vee!" Harry and Max waved at her as they followed the others out into the playground.

"Well, Vera," Miss Richards started, "Belinda—I mean Mrs Chalmers—tells me that she's entered you into the Junior School Short Story Competition. Is that right?"

Vera nodded silently.

"Is that what all the daydreaming is about this week, Vera?" she asked gently.

Vera nodded again, this time with a half-hearted smile.

"I thought as much," Miss Richards smiled back reassuringly. "That's why

I kept you back for detention. So you could start to get it all down, out of your head. So you can concentrate in class again."

She gave Vera a knowing look. "You know Vera, you really are a very good story writer. Mrs Chalmers wouldn't have entered you in the competition if she didn't believe in you. It's just you and Bethany from this school, you know."

Vera groaned and her shoulders slumped when she heard the name of the awful Bethany. The girl that wins everything, she thought. What chance did she stand against her? Why hadn't Mrs Chalmers mentioned it to her when she'd seen her today?

But as her thoughts turned to Bethany, her fingers once again found the pebble in her pocket. She turned it over and over. Its smoothness soothed her.

"I think I can win it," a small voice crept out of her own mouth, taking Vera by surprise. "I really think I can. The story I've got—well it's just unbelievably amazing, Miss Richards."

"I'm sure it is Vera. I'm sure it is. Why don't you get cracking on my old computer over there," she said nodding towards her desk. "And it's yours to use after school for as long as you want. Any day. You don't even have to get detention to use it!" Miss Richards beamed at Vera. "Just promise me that you'll pay attention in class from now on. Deal?"

"Oh thanks so much, Miss! Deal. Absolute deal. Mum doesn't have a computer at home and Gran's is so ancient and slow it keeps on crashing. And Max won't let anyone touch his in case they break it. This is just brilliant!"

Vera leaped out of her seat, resisting the temptation to give Miss Richards a huge hug. She plonked herself on her teacher's soft blue swivel chair, then started to type.

# 13. The Penguin Girl

Vera typed. And typed. And typed. Every day after school for a whole week, Vera would sit on Miss Richard's blue swivel chair, at her ever-so-tidy desk, and tap away at her computer.

Sometimes, her story wanted to come out of her head too quickly. But Mrs Chalmers had told her to get her ideas down on paper first. Even if it was just the odd word or drawing to help her remember all the bits and where they were meant to go.

And even though she was still a bit slow at typing, it was so much quicker and neater than handwriting. When she made a mistake or changed her mind, she would simply hit the 'backspace' button and start again. It even corrected her spelling for her. Computers were magic.

"Finished," breathed Vera with a satisfied sigh as she clicked the 'save' button and pushed her glasses back up her nose. She sat back in the swivel chair and gave herself a good stretch—like Biscuits the cat when he wakes up thought Vera, flexing her stiff fingers, pretending they were claws.

She looked at the computer screen.
The result of all her hard work stared
back at her. There it was. Her story—
'The Penguin Girl, by Vera McLuckie'.
Her actual story. About Ricky, Helen,
Henry and her. Not that anyone would
ever believe her if she told them it
was real.

She reached into the pocket of her
saggy school cardigan and began to

turn the pebble over and over, its smoothness slipping against the soft wool.

She'd kept the pebble a secret since that day in the back room of Gran's bookshop. She hadn't even shown it to Harry and Max who still thought her story was just that, a story. She was scared that their lack of belief in the story land that she'd conjured up would make her pebble lose its magic or, worse still, disappear.

And then I'll just become scared old Vera again. Not good at anything and too frightened to try. Maybe I'll show the pebble to them if I win the competition? Yes, maybe then, she thought.

She liked the feeling she got when she held the pebble in the palm of her hand. Just knowing it was there made her feel happier and more confident. She had even begun to believe in herself, like Mrs Chalmers was always talking about. The pebble went everywhere with her. She even slept with it under her pillow.

Harry and Max had noticed a change in Vera too, since 'The Day of the Story' as they now called it. And it was quite something for Max to notice someone else's feelings.

"You're really smiley at the moment, Vera," he had said one day at break time. "It suits you."

"Yeh Vee, this writing thing is really

good for you," Harry had added, throwing her arms around both her friends' shoulders and slapping them on the back—hard! (Sometimes Harry didn't know her own strength.) "Even though we haven't been able to do the Daydream Club for a week now, it's been worth it to see you so happy," she had smiled.

Even Mum and Gran had noticed the difference in her. Getting up for school in the morning. Easier. Getting dressed for school in the morning. Quicker. Number of days she'd told Gran that she'd enjoyed school. Five out of five. Number of times she'd complained to Mum about her spending too much time at work. None. She'd even tried Gran's homemade lasagne last night— which was amazing as Vera had insisted on sausages, rice and peas for dinner every night for the last five years.

But now it was quiet. The school was always so peaceful at this time of day, once everyone had gone home. Vera loved the sound of silence. The horrible bell to mark the end of the school day had rung over an hour ago.

Vera was so excited she'd finished her story and printed it all by herself that she decided to go and see if Mrs Chalmers was still around. Sometimes Mrs Chalmers stayed late, catching up on marking or waiting for Bethany to finish one of her many after school clubs. Bethany went to loads of clubs and was, naturally, fabulous at them all.

Vera skipped along the corridor, waving her arms around like a windmill. "I'm finished! I'm finished! I'm finished!" sang Vera. "I'm finished! I'm finished! I'm fin ..."

Bang! Vera had been so busy skipping, flapping and singing that she hadn't seen someone standing outside Mrs Chalmers' classroom and had run headlong into them. Unfortunately, that someone was Bethany.

"Well, well!" sneered Bethany. "Look who it is. Vera McLuckie. Or perhaps I should call you Vera Not-So-Lucky."

Bethany smirked as she looked down at the pile of paper—Vera's story—that now lay across the corridor floor along with Vera. "Is that your story for the competition?" she asked. "I bet it's utter rubbish."

Vera scrambled to her knees and frantically started picking up all the bits of paper. Her happy feeling had gone. She felt sick and began to shake with fear. The words on the pages in front of her began to blur as she tried to fight back her tears.

"Sorry," she mumbled. "Sorry, Bethany."

"I should think so too," sneered Bethany. "Always so clumsy, Vera. At least you didn't knock your glasses off this time," she laughed. A cruel laugh, not a funny one.

"Always ... Hmm, what's this?" Bethany stooped to pick something up off the floor. Something small and smooth that had fallen out of Vera's pocket and skidded under the radiator in the narrow corridor.

"Leave that alone!" Vera exploded suddenly, jumping up, her face as bright red as her glasses. Her whole body shook, but now it was with anger.

She stood facing Bethany, her fists clenched in tight balls. "Give it back! It's mine!" she demanded.

"Poor little Vera," said Bethany cruelly. She pushed Vera's hand away each time she tried to make a grab for her pebble. Bethany was so much taller and stronger than Vera.

"Lost something precious? What is it anyway?" she said looking down. "Just some useless stone." That cruel laugh again.

Then she began to chant, "Vera's lost her stone! Vera's lost her stone! Vera's lost her stone!" as she held Vera's treasure high in the air. So high that Vera couldn't reach it even when she jumped.

"Give it back! Give it back!" Vera yelled, jumping and grabbing, trying to snatch the pebble from Bethany's hand. "It's my pebble! You don't understand."

By now Vera was shaking uncontrollably and had started to cry big tears, gulping as great fat drops ran down her face. Her whole body felt hot. Then cold. Then hot again.

She began to feel light. But not in that nice way like when she'd been telling the story to Harry and Max before they'd started to fly. No. This was a horrible lightness, like the earth was trying to swallow her whole.

The last thing Vera remembered, before it all went dark and she fell to the ground, was the sound of a door opening and Mrs Chalmers' voice— angry and hard, not soft and calm as normal— saying, "Bethany! What on earth have you done?"

# 14. A change of heart

"It's all your fault! I hate you!"

Vera opened her eyes to the sound of Bethany screeching and shouting. But not at her this time. At her mum, Mrs Chalmers.

Vera realised she was still lying on the floor of the corridor outside Mrs Chalmers' office and that only seconds had passed since she'd fallen and it had all gone dark. Still clutching her story tightly in one hand, she reached up to her eyes with her other. Yes. Thankfully her glasses were still there in one piece.

"It's you. You've made everything bad. You made me this way," Bethany continued, her voice getting louder. "You even made dad leave. The only reason I do all this stuff—all these stupid competitions—is to make him proud of me so he'll come back. But he doesn't, does he? And he isn't, is he? So what's the point?"

Bethany's voice began to wobble and her face crumpled, "Can't you see I'm unhappy?" Bethany looked at her mum with big pleading eyes, tears beginning to slide down her face, "You're so busy helping everyone else that you never notice me. I need help too."

"Oh, my dear," Mrs
Chalmers soothed,
"come here." She took
Bethany in her arms,
hugging her gently,
smoothing her hair
and whispering, "I'm
sorry. I'm sorry," over
and over again.

Vera sat up against
the wall and gave a gentle cough
to remind them she was still there,
listening.

"Oh, Vera my love. Are you OK?" Mrs
Chalmers looked up, cradling Bethany
in her arms, rocking her to and fro.

"My dad isn't around either Bethany,"
Vera began in her quiet voice. "It's
not easy, is it? I didn't even know
him but I miss him. I really do," she
sighed. "And I know my mum does too.
I hear her crying some nights when I'm
in bed and she thinks I'm asleep. It
makes me feel sad."

Bethany stopped sobbing into her
mum's shoulder and looked at Vera. It
was a look of utter amazement. Like
she was seeing Vera for the very first
time.

"I had no idea," she said in a whisper,
wiping the tears away from her face
with the back of her hand. "Thanks
Vera. Thanks for being so kind.
Especially when I've been so mean to
you."

She looked at Vera with a sad smile, adding sheepishly, "I'm really, really sorry." And with that, Bethany stretched out her hand to help Vera up off the floor. "Here's your stone. It obviously means a lot to you. I'm so sorry I took it. I'm so sorry you fell. Are you OK?"

Vera took her pebble from Bethany and slipped it into her cardigan pocket. Safe and sound. Her fingers curled around it and she began to feel the familiar warm glow—a happy feeling—travelling through her whole body.

Before she knew what she was doing

she had thrown her arms around Bethany and Mrs Chalmers, giving them the most enormous hug.

"It's OK," said Vera, "my mum says that everyone finds life tricky sometimes. That's why we should always be good to each other."

"She's a wise lady, your mum," smiled Mrs Chalmers, giving Vera a reassuring squeeze. "Bethany love, can you give me five minutes with Vera then we can head off home for tea. I think we've got a lot more talking to do, don't you?"

"Yes, we do," nodded Bethany slowly, smiling a sad smile at her mum as she wiped the last of her tears away from her face.

Mrs Chalmers handed her a tissue which had been tucked up her sleeve, and Bethany gave her nose an enormous blow.

"I'll wait here," she added turning to Vera. "And thanks. Thanks for everything." Bethany gave Vera a big hug and a genuinely warm smile.

A slightly stunned Vera smiled back (Bethany Chalmers, being nice to her?) and followed Mrs Chalmers into her classroom.

Mrs Chalmers gently shut the door behind them. "Well," she said with a rather large sigh, "that seems to have cleared the air a bit. And thanks for being so understanding Vera. I do hope you didn't hurt yourself when you fell."

"No, I'm fine thanks. Honest," Vera smiled back. She stretched out the hand that was still tightly gripping her story and offered it to Mrs Chalmers.

"Here," she said with a hint of nerves, "I've finished. That's why I was racing round here. That's why I bumped into Bethany. I was so excited I just had to show it to you. To see what you thought. It's called 'The Penguin Girl'. And I typed it and printed it all by myself," she added proudly.

"Vera, why don't you go with Bethany to get a drink of water while I read this?" said Mrs Chalmers as she took the pile of crumpled paper from Vera and perched herself on the edge of her desk.

☹☺☺

As Vera returned to the classroom, she fumbled nervously with the pebble in her pocket. What if Mrs Chalmers doesn't like my story, she thought?

"Vera," said Mrs Chalmers looking up as she entered the room, "look at me."

Vera looked Mrs Chalmers straight in the eye, something that would normally have felt too uncomfortable for her to do.

"It's a winner," Mrs Chalmers said slowly.

Vera gaped back at her, her mouth wide open.

"It's absolutely brilliant Vera McLuckie. So you can take that worried look off your face right now!" Mrs Chalmers beamed a broad smile that lit up Vera's heart.

"Really?" whispered Vera. "I thought it was good, but ... well ... you never know," her voice trailed off.

"Well it is good. Very good," said Mrs Chalmers reassuringly. "And I do know that this, my dear, is a winner. Now all we need to do is get it off to the competition. And then wait."

# 15. Vee and Bee

*Sorry I haven't dropped by for a while to see how you're doing. You see, I just got totally caught up in Vera's story. No, not that one. Not 'The Penguin Girl', although it is amazing and quite brilliant (and of course, as both you and I know, absolutely not a story and very, very true). No, the story of Vera and Bethany.*

*Who would have thought that someone as cool, elegant and clever as Bethany*

Chalmers, the all-round bestest being at Acorn Bank Primary, had problems? That even she felt sad and angry about things sometimes. That actually she and Vera had more in common than either of them had known.

In the days that followed, they discovered two more things they had in common. Number One, they both hated waiting—two weeks they had to wait until the results of the story competition were announced. And Number Two, they actually liked each other!

# 16. And the winner is ...

It was a beautiful sunny morning.
Vera, Harry and Max—The Daydream
Club—stood in their playground
huddle, waiting for the bell to ring and
another school day to begin.

Max pulled at the peak of his cap,
shielding his eyes from the sun's rays.
He really didn't like summer, it was
simply too bright and far too hot.

"Hey Vera! Hey guys!" Bethany

bounded up to them, her perfect blonde plait swinging behind her. "Have you heard anything yet? About the competition?"

Vera shook her head. "Nope. I'm beginning to get a bit worried actually," she added with a yawn. Vera was a worrier at the best of times. But with the added stress of the story competition hanging over her, she hadn't been sleeping at all well recently.

Only last night she'd woken up in a panic after a horrible nightmare. She, along with the three penguins—Ricky, Helen and Henry—were being chased around the zoo by a giant angry kookaburra who kept on laughing at them. She'd been so scared, she'd had

to slip into bed beside her mum and
Biscuits the cat to get back to sleep.

"Don't worry Vera," Bethany placed
a careful hand on her new friend's
shoulder, "I haven't heard anything
either. Maybe today, huh?"

Bethany spied her mum heading across
the playground. She smiled and waved.
"Anyway, must dash. See you in
class." And with that she trotted off
in the direction of Mrs Chalmers.

"Wowee!" whistled Harry. "I can't believe how much she's changed. What on earth did you do to her Vee?" she laughed.

"I guess we just realised that maybe we're not so different after all," Vera shrugged, smiling. "But you're still my two best friends in the world. Ever." Vera put her arms around Harry and Max and gave them both a tight squeeze.

The school bell rang out and they began to make their way steadily towards Miss Richard's classroom.

"I don't know," said Max warily. "I don't understand how someone can change so quickly. One day horrible, the next day all smiley and friendly.

How does that happen?"

"I guess it just does," said Vera. "People do change. We all change, all the time."

"Yeh," added Harry. "Just look at you Vera. Ever since that day at Dog-Eared Books when you told us your amazing story, you've been so much happier. So much braver. You've got so much more get up and go. Crikey, you even entered a writing competition!"

Harry kept on talking but Vera had stopped listening. All she could think about as she walked through the door of Room 24 was the large brown envelope sitting

Vera
McLuckie

there on her desk. Addressed in big bold letters to her. She froze.

"Go on, open it Vee," nudged Harry as she and Max hovered beside her.

Miss Richards sidled over too, smiling, "Open it, Vera," she said nodding encouragingly.

"Here goes," whispered Vera, slowly sliding out a single piece of thick paper from the envelope. The words, in fancy green print, danced before her eyes as she silently mouthed them.

Congratulations VERA McLUCKIE
You have been awarded

FIRST PRIZE

in the Oakchester Junior Schools
Short Story Competition

"Oh!" Vera let out a tiny squeak, her eyes wide behind her glasses. "Oh!" she squeaked again, "I've done it!"

She looked up to find the whole class crowded around her, peering over each other's shoulders to see if they could read what was on the bit of paper. The Certificate. For First Prize. First in the whole of the Oakchester Junior Schools Short Story Competition.

"I've done it!" she shouted, jumping up and down, smiling ear to ear, "I got first prize!"

Harry lunged at Vera, nearly knocking her over, and gave her the most enormous bear hug. The girls started to jump up and down, wearing huge grins. Even Max joined in, his hat joggling on his head as he bounced along with the girls.

An enormous cheer went up from the rest of the class as they began to chant, "Vera! Vera! Vera!" led by Bethany, who stood at the front of the group conducting them like an orchestra.

Vera looked up, amazed, still grinning from ear to ear.

Bethany beamed back. "Well done Vera! You deserved to win. I know how hard you worked on this and how good your story was. I came second," she said, waving her certificate at Vera without a hint of showing off. "And I'm so pleased, for both of us."

☺☺☺

The rest of the day went by in a bit of a blur for Vera. Like one enormous daydream. She kept on reading the words on the certificate over and over. She simply couldn't believe what had happened.

Even when assembly came around and her name was called out by a very happy Mr Gibson

to go on stage and collect her prize from an even happier Mrs Chalmers. Even when she was standing side by side with Bethany in front of the whole school listening to their loud clapping and cheering. But it had happened. She had won. She was a winner.

"So what did you win then, Vee?" asked Harry.

Harry, Max and Vera were all sitting around the table in the back room of Dog-Eared Books, excitedly going over the days' events. Gran had switched on an old electric fan for them before they had arrived to try and cool the room down. It had gradually got hotter and hotter during the day and nobody wanted to open the windows because of the fishy smell outside. Shakespeare lay panting in the corner, flopped on the cool floor.

"I haven't even looked," said Vera a bit embarrassed. Her eyes quickly scanned the other bits of paper that had come in the envelope with the certificate.

"Oh, this is too funny!" she laughed. "You'll never guess. I've won tickets to London Zoo! Three children plus two adults. So that's me and you two," she said pointing at Max and Harry. "Plus mum and Gran."

"Brilliant!" said Harry. "Can we go and see the penguins? Like the ones in your story?"

"And can we get the Number 274 bus?" added Max.

"Of course we can," laughed Vera. "But first ..." she paused, "I have something to tell you both. Something important. Very important," she said suddenly coming over all serious. "The reason why I won."

"Vee, you won because it was the best story," Harry chipped in.

"Well yes. And no," added Vera.

"You're talking in riddles again Vera," said Max. "Please explain."

"OK," said Vera slowly. Despite it being such a hot day, Vera was still wearing her favourite cardigan. She reached a hand into its saggy pocket and pulled out the small white pebble, laying it on the table in front of an astonished Harry and Max. "It's because of this ..."

# 17. Being extra-ordinary

"Where did you get that Vee?" asked Harry, slowly. "It looks exactly like the pebble Ricky the Rockhopper gave you." She cleared her throat, "I mean, when you were telling us your story that's how I imagined it looked. Exactly."

Vera looked Harry straight in the eye and said very seriously, "That's because it is, Harry. This is the pebble that Ricky gave me."

"What? You mean ... What?" Harry shook her head in disbelief.

"Oh, I see," said Max, nodding as if he had just solved a giant puzzle—like the ones he loved so much in his Bumper Book of Puzzles. "I couldn't work out why your story seemed so real Vera. But now it all makes perfect sense. It's because it was real." He laughed, "Genius. Pure genius. You really are something special Vera, aren't you?"

"Um, I guess so," Vera agreed reluctantly. "But that day in Dog-Eared Books when I told you the story, well that was the easy bit—to make a story so real that it comes to life. But it was this," she said holding out the pebble in the palm of her hand, "that made me feel the way I did afterwards. That made me believe I could write the story. That helped me to get it all down on paper. It even gave me the courage to make friends with Bethany."

"It's magic, you see," she went on, "and the only reason I haven't shown it to you until now is I knew you'd think I'd just made everything up. I thought the pebble's special powers would simply run out if you saw it when you didn't believe. Sorry." Vera sighed and looked down at the table.

"Vera McLuckie," Harry stood up her full height, towering over her tiny friend and looked at her crossly, as cross as Harry could get anyway.

"Now you listen to me. The only thing that's magic around here is you. Not that pebble," she said jabbing her finger at where the pebble nestled in Vera's hand.

"It was you who made all of this happen. All by yourself. Every single bit. You even made that," she waggled her finger, "silly pebble real."

"Max is right, you know, you really are something special. You even said so yourself, in your story. That we're all extraordinary in our own way, remember? And I think you've just shown us, and yourself, and everybody else who knows you just how extraordinary you really are. Not that pebble."

Vera smiled and nodded slowly. She gave the pebble one last glance before slipping it back into her pocket.

"OK, you're right. I give in," she laughed, shrugging her shoulders. "I am extraordinary, aren't I? I guess the difference is that now I believe it and I like it. I like being me. I like the bits that make me different. I love you guys for the same reason. And I love our Daydream Club."

She beamed at her friends, "But if it's alright with you, I think I'll hang onto the pebble for a while longer. You see I like the way it feels in my pocket. It might not be magic after all, but it's good at reminding me that I am!"

"Now," she looked up at Harry and Max, "shall we plan our trip to the zoo?"

# 18. Guess who?

*So that's it. The story of Vera McLuckie and the Daydream Club. I hope you enjoyed it.*

*But before I go, I think I've got some explaining to do. You may well have been thinking to yourself as you've been reading, who on earth is that person who's been interrupting a perfectly good story all the way through? I do hope I haven't been too annoying. But I wonder, have you guessed?*

I'll give you a clue—just the one though. I'm sitting here tapping away at my computer, writing. And on my desk is a smooth white pebble, because that's still the way I write after all this time.

That's right. It's me! I'm Vera! A bit older (quite a bit actually). I don't wear glasses anymore. I've got these funny jelly-like things called contact lenses that are pretty tricky to put in my eyes every morning. But they are brilliant at helping me see. And I still like wearing comfy clothes. Saggy cardigans are my absolute favourite. My writing is still a mess and I still daydream a lot. An awful lot in fact.

*But none of these things have stopped me from writing this book. Vera McLuckie and the Daydream Club. A story of friendship, differences, penguins and a little girl with a huge imagination. And, most important of all, it's a story of believing in yourself no matter what. Because we all have a magical power inside us. It's just that sometimes we need to be brave enough to take the first step. To give things a try. Then we get to find out where our magic really lies.*

*Take the rest of the Daydream Club for example. Did you guess that Harry did all of the illustrations in this book? I told you she was brilliant at drawing. She's an artist now and still loves to swim, although not at the same time*

as drawing as that would be very silly
indeed.

And Max? Well Max is busy being
brilliant in California, U.S. of A. (that's
Max's way of saying the United States
of America), doing very clever stuff
with computers. He still wears a hat
every day. Everywhere.

But that's all about now. And there's still so much to tell you about then. About the extraordinary Vera and her wonderful friends and her amazing talent for making her stories come to life. Another day perhaps?

# WIN A PRIZE!

*Your mission is to find the hidden penguins to unlock the code word.*

There are 15 hidden teeny tiny penguins inside the book that look like the penguin on Vera's pyjamas on the first page of the story

Things you will need

pencil and paper

calculator

big person

(16 if you count that one). Follow the steps below.

**1.** *Write* down the **page number of every illustration** that contains a tiny hidden penguin. (Hint: remember there are just 15.)

**2.** Now *circle* just the **Unit** (as in Hundreds, Tens and Units) of each page number you wrote down (e.g. circle 5 if you found one on page 25, and 3 if you found one on page 153).

**3.** *Add* together all the numbers you circled and *write* this number down with a square around it. (Hint: use a calculator if you find the sum too difficult.)

**4.** *Subtract* 2 from the number you wrote down in the square and *write* down the answer in a triangle.

**5.** *Count* all the letters in the title of the book then *subtract* 5. Draw an arrow next to that number.

**6.** *Turn* to the page in the book you wrote down in the triangle. Count the words from the beginning of the page until you get to the number you wrote next to the arrow. *You are on the code word!*

**7.** *Type* the following in a web browser: **www.yourstoriesmatter.org/** followed by the code word (e.g. if the code word is cat, you would type www.yourstoriesmatter.org/cat).

**8.** If you worked out everything correctly, you will be taken to a special hidden web page. Keep this to yourself — it's your prize!

If there are any prizes left, you will be able to choose one! If not, you're definitely a winner for trying it anyway, so don't worry, be happy ☺

www.**YourStoriesMatter**.org

sharing experiences | improving understanding | celebrating differences

# YOUR STORIES MATTER

**We are independent educational book publishers**
set up for social rather than financial profit:

*collecting*
inspiring stories
from around the world

*publishing*
books for schools and families
dealing with specific learning difficulties

*producing*
free teaching resources
that can be used with our books

## YOU CAN JOIN US

*as a user*
of our resources to help spread well-being

*as a contributor*
of resources and stories to inspire others

*as a champion*
helping us to curate and promote info on your chosen topic

**www.yourstoriesmatter.org**

# Some other books available from
# YOUR STORIES
# MATTER

**You're So Clumsy Charley:** This illustrated children's story (aged 6-8) explains what it feels like to be a child who is different from other children. Charley seems to keep getting into trouble all the time for doing things wrong. While not labelled in the story, Charley has a specific learning difficulty. When Charley learns he is not alone, things begin to get better for him.

**Emily's Sister:** A story told from the point of view of a child wanting to know more about how Dyspraxia and SPD affects her sister. This children's story, based on real events, paves the way for parents, teachers and medical professionals to discuss these specific learning difficulties with children (aged around 7-9).

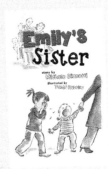

**The Back to Front World of Azzie Artbuckle:** This illustrated children's story explains what it feels like to be a child who finds it difficult to read. When Azzie discovers she has Dyslexia, life begins to get easier for her and everyone around her. This book can be used to gently discuss Dyslexia and related learning difficulties with children aged 6-8.

## Check them out at
## www.**YourStoriesMatter**.org